DATE DUE		
SEP 27 1984		AUG 1 1 2007
FEB 0 1 1990		NOV 1 5 2007
AUG 0 4 1990	SEP 2 8 1990	JAN 0 4 2003
FEB 2 8 2000		
NOV 0 1 2009		

THE FRIENDS OF ABU ALI

Three More Tales of the Middle East

Ready-to-Read

THE FRIENDS OF ABU ALI

Three More Tales of the Middle East
Retold by Dorothy O. Van Woerkom
Illustrated by Harold Berson

MACMILLAN PUBLISHING CO., INC.
New York
COLLIER MACMILLAN PUBLISHERS
London

Copyright © 1978 Dorothy O. Van Woerkom
Copyright © 1978 Harold Berson

Macmillan Publishing Co., Inc.
866 Third Avenue, New York, N.Y. 10022
Collier Macmillan Canada, Ltd.

Printed in the United States of America

10 9 8 7 6 5 4 3 2 1

LIBRARY OF CONGRESS CATALOGING IN PUBLICATION DATA

Van Woerkom, Dorothy.
 The friends of Abu Ali.

 (Ready-to-read)
 SUMMARY: Retells three more adventures of muddleheaded
Abu Ali including "The Bag of Rice," "Cake for Sale," and
"The Donkey's Shadow."
 1. Tales, Turkish. [1. Folklore—Turkey] I. Berson, Harold.
II. Title.   PZ8.1.V457Fr   1978   [398.2] [E]   77-12624
ISBN 0-02-791320-1

*These stories
are freely adapted
from tales told of
Nasr-ed-Din Hodja, one
of the most celebrated
personalities of
the Middle East.*

For Mary Blount Christian

Contents

The Bag of Rice

Abu Ali
put a pot of water
on the stove.

He looked into
his rice barrel.
No rice!

"I will ask
friend Nouri,"
Abu Ali said.
"He will give me
some rice."

11

It was not far

to Nouri's house.

Nouri said,
"Oh, Ali!"
He put some rice
in a big bag.
"You are always
running out of things."
"I do not mean
to run out,"
Abu Ali said.
"I just forget
to buy more."

Abu Ali
was walking home
with his bag of rice.
He met Hamid
and Musa.

"Did you
    run out of rice
      again?" Musa asked.
"I did,"
    said Abu Ali.
"But when I
    get rich
    I will never
    run out of rice!"

Hamid said,
"When I get rich
I will buy
lots of land."
"When I get rich,"
said Musa,
"I will buy
a dozen donkeys."

Soon they came
to a bridge.
Hamid said,
"I will buy this bridge
when I get rich."

Then Musa
began to run.
He made sounds
like a donkey.
"Eee-aww!"

"Watch out, Hamid!"
he said.
"My dozen donkeys
are going to cross
your bridge!"

But Hamid
got there first.
"I am sorry, Musa,"
he said.
"Your donkeys
cannot cross
my bridge."

This made Musa
very angry.
"I want to get
to the other side,"
he said to Hamid.
"My donkeys
must go too.
How can I
leave them here?"

Hamid crossed his arms.
"No donkeys
on my bridge,"
he said.

"What silly friends
you are!"
said Abu Ali.
"Hamid, you have
no bridge.
Musa, you have
no donkeys."

Abu Ali
took his bag
of rice.
He turned it
upside down.
All the rice
fell into the water.

He said,
"Do you see
what is
in this bag?
NOTHING!
Your two heads
are like this rice bag.
THERE IS NOTHING
IN THEM!"

Cake for
Sale

Abu Ali
went to
Hamid's house.

"Shhhh!" said Hamid.
"My cake is
in the oven.
Be careful!
It may fall."

"How good it smells!"
said Abu Ali.
"I will wait
until your cake
is done."

"Friend Ali," Hamid said,
"this cake is not to eat.
It is for sale.
I am taking it
to the fair tomorrow."

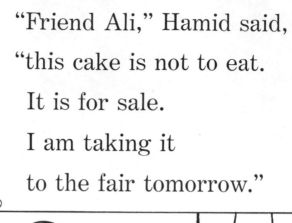

Abu Ali said,
"Tomorrow you can
sell the cake.
Today I want to
smell it."
"Smell," said Hamid.
"But while you are
smelling,
you can help me
wash the dishes."

Soon Hamid said,

"The time is up.

My cake is done."

He took the cake

out of the oven.

"Oh, dear!" he said.

Hamid's cake

had fallen

in the middle.

"Too bad,"
said Abu Ali.
"Now we will
have to eat it."

But Hamid said,
"YOU did it, Ali!
You made my cake fall!
You smelled
and smelled
and kept on
smelling it.
All that smelling
made my cake fall!"

"I am sorry, Hamid,"
Abu Ali said.
"I will pay you
for the cake."
He took some pennies
from his pocket.

PLINK!

PLINK!

PLINK! PLINK! PLINK!

Abu Ali

dropped the pennies

on the table.

Then he picked

them up again.

"Why did you do that?"

asked Hamid.

"Did you hear
the pennies, Hamid?"
Abu Ali asked.
"Of course
I heard them,"
Hamid said.
"That is good,"
said Abu Ali.
"Now your pockets
must be full
of pennies."

Hamid turned his pockets
inside out.
"I have nothing
in my pockets."

Abu Ali laughed.

He said, "Friend Hamid,

if smelling cake

will make it fall,

then hearing

pennies plink

will fill your pockets!"

This time
Hamid laughed.
"Ali, you are right,"
he said. "When you
smelled my cake,
you did not
make it fall."

Abu Ali took
the mixing bowl.
He said to Hamid,
"Let us eat
the fallen cake.
And I will help you
bake one for the fair."

They mixed a cake
and put it
in the oven.
Hamid made some tea.
They drank the tea
and ate the fallen cake.

Then Hamid said,
"The time is up.
   Our new cake is done."
He took the cake
out of the oven.

"Oh!" said Abu Ali.
"That is a fine cake."
"How high it is,"
   said Hamid.

"Do you know why
that cake is high?"
asked Abu Ali.
"When that cake
was in the oven,
I was careful
not to smell it!"

The Donkey's Shadow

"Friend Ali,"
   Nouri said,
"take this money.
   I want to rent
   your donkey."

"What for?"
   asked Abu Ali.
   Nouri said,
"My donkey is
   at my uncle's house.
   I am going there
   to get it."

Abu Ali said,
"Friend Nouri,
I will take you there
for nothing."
"Please, Ali,"
Nouri said,
"I really want to
pay you."

"Then get up
behind me,"
Abu Ali said.
He put the money
in his pocket.
"Whr-r-r-r!"
he said to his
donkey.

For a long time
they rode
in the hot sun.
"I did not know
your uncle lived
so far away,"
Abu Ali said.

At last
they stopped to rest.
Nouri sat down
in the donkey's shadow.

"Move over, Nouri,"
  Abu Ali said.
"It is hot in the sun."
"I am sorry,"
  Nouri said.
"There is no room."

"No room?"
yelled Abu Ali.
"I think I can sit
in the shadow
of my own donkey!"
"You can sit here
tomorrow," Nouri said.
"Today I am renting
this donkey."

Abu Ali was hot.

He was cross.

"You are renting

this DONKEY,"

he shouted.

"But you are not renting

this donkey's SHADOW."

He pulled the donkey,

and the shadow moved.

"A donkey's shadow
is part of himself!"
Nouri shouted back.
"Everybody knows that."

He pulled the donkey,

and the shadow

moved again.

"Well, I do not know it,"
Abu Ali said.
"I would never rent
my donkey's shadow."
He pulled the donkey,
and the shadow moved.

58

Nouri waved
his arms around.
"If you did not
want to rent it,
you should have
made the donkey
leave it at home,"
he said.

"Eeeee-awwww!"
said the donkey,
and he ran back
down the road.

"Now see what
you have done!"
Abu Ali said.
"We have no shadow
and we have
no donkey!"

"Never mind,"
Nouri said.
"We are almost at
my uncle's house.
You can rent
MY donkey,
and I will help you
look for yours."

Abu Ali laughed
and gave the money
back to Nouri.
"Here is my rent,
friend Nouri," he said.
"Something tells me
we are bigger donkeys
than the one
that ran away!"